Scruffy

The True Tale of an Orphan Doggie

by
Susan
Corning

Illustrations by
Christine Eyer

Book One: *Colombia*

The Scruffy Saga Press

2020

This book is dedicated to
Anna Renée Neese,
who loved all creatures,
great and small.
1978–2004

CHAPTER ONE

"We can have food, and we can have love.
Sometimes it's hard to tell which is which..."
~ Scruffy *(Kampala, Uganda, 2013)*

Scruffy Leaves the Farm

Colombia, November, 2006

Soldiers slip through the withering grasses in the face of impending winter. Under cover of darkness, they move forward with purpose, following El Jefe's silent signals. In combat fatigues and gear, with blackened faces, they are night stalking. Only their eyes are seen, glittering with the prospect of a mission, an assured small victory that will ultimately serve their larger plan and purpose.

It is cold in autumn in the *Nevado del Huilla* and the winds pour over the highland meadows with icy breath from surrounding snow-covered peaks. My memory of those days has faded. Autumn was when the soldiers came and we left our little farm.

I do remember the warmth of my mummy in the box stall where Jacobo, the burro slept at night. He was very kind. He welcomed the company and was careful not to step on one little, squirming female pup—me.

At night, my siblings and I curled up next to mummy's belly, fighting for the closest spot. We had no food from her in those days. Not that we were too old for that, but mummy was tired, and her ribs were sharply outlined under her dull, patchy coat. She had seen many seasons by then and besides, she didn't have enough to eat herself. So, we fed on scraps we stole from the chickens, the pig, even Jacobo, and sometimes a crust of delicious bread snuck over by Marta, the little girl from the big stall where the family lived. We were always a little hungry but warm and oh, so jolly!

The night the soldiers came we learned firsthand about cold. My brothers and sisters and I were sound asleep, except Carlitos, who was stalking a shadow he imagined was a mouse. He was the biggest of of us all and often hunted on his own, even at the age of 12 weeks. If we had stayed on the farm, he would have been a sure survivor of our little family, but when the soldiers came, he ran out into the yard barking and growling threats and insults, so they shot him.

Mummy woke up and told us all to run as fast and as far as we could go, and not all in the same direction or in one group. She waited until we scampered off—it took a few growls for us to realize she was serious—and then she followed where Carlitos had run outside, but she headed straight and silently to the leg of one of the soldiers, sinking teeth into flesh. I didn't see, but I heard the shouts, the sound of metal hitting flesh, a yelp, more growls, and finally the gunshot that killed her.

I was little—they called me the "runt"—and weak. Plus, I was and am a scaredy-cat. Instead of running into the brush with my brothers and sisters, I hid behind the harvest sack, shivering with fear, whimpering at the sudden loss. I never saw any of my birth family again.

I scrunched to a very little pup, 'cause the soldiers were tromping through the barn shoving Marta's papa ahead of them. They demanded that Rafael turn over the keys to the storehouse lock. He shook his head, and they kicked him to the ground.

I could see Jacobo in his little stall with hay in his mouth, but he was no longer munching. He moved uneasily, ears flickering to catch the sounds. Rafael groaned. "*Es que no hay llaves.*" He pushed open the door with his foot and, lo and behold, the storehouse door opened. No need for keys!

Unsurprisingly, the storehouse was empty after a bad year and depleted harvest stocks. I was hiding behind the last sack of grain in the barn! Uh oh! A soldier lifted the bag and slung it over his shoulder.

I was exposed to the eyes of the small group of men. I was done for, except that Jacobo, eyes and ears now fully attentive to the soldier's rough and rude movements, began to bray, *hee haw hee haw hee haw*— deafening at the best of times, maddening at the worst. The soldiers, distracted, looked over at the skinny old burro. One of the soldiers toyed with his gun and I thought for certain he would shoot my friend. Finally though, the man snorted, "*No vale ni una bala ni llevarlo…* no use to us, not even worth a bullet!" This gave me a moment to wriggle into a very small space behind the straw and empty sacks.

The soldiers hauled Rafael and the last sack of grain out the door and I skedaddled into Jacobo's stall, hiding under the pile of straw that was his last meal at that sad farm.

The family from the big stall packed their belongings to leave the land they and their grandparents and great-grandparents had farmed since the days from beyond time's remembrance. Somewhere in that process, Marta, the littlest girl-child, scooped me up (I admit I was still whimpering in fear of the soldiers) and placed me inside her shawl.

She hugged it tightly to her little body. Then the family, including Jacobo—loaded with the family's selected belongings—began the long journey to the noisy, dirty place of cars and lights and hard roads.

The journey took months and there are many stories between then and now. I was so small that Marta hid me for most of that time. When her mummy found me just before we entered Bogota (that's what they called the noisy place), Marta cried so hard when they tried to take me away that her mummy said okay, but that I would die anyway from lack of food. Marta cried all the harder and at supper gave me her bread when her mummy wasn't looking. As delicious as the bread was, equally so were the tears I licked off of Marta's face.

Bread and tears were mostly all we ate in those days. It seems amazing that bread alone could give me enough energy to walk at the heels of my little friend. Now, I understand that she walked slowly like her mummy and her two brothers because they didn't know where they were going or, worse, what they would do when they got to the unknown place.

Everything they now owned was on the back of Jacobo or strapped across the shoulders of the two brothers. Where Marta's daddy had gone, I did not know, and his name was only spoken once, when Marta's mummy moaned in her sleep one night. "*Rafael,*" she said as she turned over and hugged her daughter and me close in her dream state. I suspect he was taken by the soldiers, one way or the other.

CHAPTER TWO

Scruffy Begins a New Life in the City

Poor old Jacobo was shuffling along, slower and slower. Sometimes the oldest brother had to smack his behind to get him to move at all. Jacobo wasn't stubborn as everyone says burros tend to be, just very tired and also old. He longed for the stall with golden straw that brought warmth and rest. But the older brother told him the little barn was gone and the land no longer theirs—lost into the hands of the soldiers. The brother said they could never go back. After hearing that, Jacobo seemed to not be concerned if he was smacked on the rump or yelled at to hurry up. His loppy, funny ears we used to chew on with pesky milk teeth flopped up and down beside his big brown eyes as if he didn't care to hear or see where he was going.

The family sold him first when we got to the city. We came down the narrow road from La Calera into Bogota, where we passed many *talleres*, the workshops along the way, and the brothers asked each one if they wanted to buy something—a pot or a pan—since these were men who made or sold things. Jacobo was apparently the only item of value and I watched him walk away with his new owner, ears drooping and eyes half-closed in sorrow.

His new owner was dressed fairly well, better than my family, and had the tools of a carpenter on his shoulder, which he loaded onto Jacobo's back. My friend looked over at us only once, but his new owner shouted and then Jacobo looked straight ahead, marching one foot in front of the other. After that he never turned around. I know because I watched with great interest, looking for a sign to run and yip at his heels, hoping to play as we used to on the farm.

Marta finally picked me up and said not to worry, Jacobo was going to a better home, and then she fed me a crust of bread.

It's hard to lose so many things when you're little.

After Jacobo, the family started selling all their pots, extra clothes, and even their few blankets. Her mummy kept only one tattered blanket to cover my Marta, who was by now very skinny.

In the city of Bogota it was winter and rain fell almost every day and every night. The cold coaxed energy from us and we had little food to fuel our bodies. Even so, I remember with longing how I crept under Marta's thin blanket to lie in a half-moon next to her chest and belly. She would clasp me to her breast and curl her little body around mine. Thus, we both slept that dreamy sleep of innocence, bathed in a shared warmth that slowed our shivering.

For a long time we lived on a street sidewalk of grey, cold concrete. Marta's mummy said we were lucky, because we were near many cafes and a bakery with Very Useful Trash. In that trash, we found pieces of food, but especially cardboard boxes the brothers made into sleeping shelters against the rain and cold. I didn't feel lucky, though, because I still remembered our lives at the farm.

One night, a little boy and girl came by to look in our trash bin. I was very surprised to see the brothers leap to their feet brandishing sharp metal pieces that glinted under the streetlamp. They snarled warnings and jabbed aggressively with their fists, and those kids ran off!

I whimpered because I remembered that had happened to us before we found our own corner, and I could smell fear in the air. The same thing happened if a stray dog came around. Always hoping to see one of my birth family, I would run out, tail wagging, only to be met by growls and then the shouts of the brothers.

After a stray ran away, the brothers hollered at me because I wasn't a good "guard" dog, and said I was useless and should be sent away, too. I tried to be more of a guard dog and learned to raise the hair on the back of my neck and attempted scary snarls. At least that made Marta laugh, which she did little of in those days.

I was getting bigger and bigger while Marta seemed to get smaller and smaller. She snuck scraps of bread to me when she could, but I needed more. In true fear and at first, trembling, I began to sniff through the trash bin when the family was at work. A whole new world opened up to me! I found pieces of bone with meat on it, cartons with drops of yogurt in the bottom, and bread that was so much more than that, with cheese, pieces of meat and some kind of oil. Mmmmm! That was delicious! I began to appreciate the "luck" of living on that corner!

One afternoon I got a little carried away having a feast at the bottom of the bin—yogurt drops, a chicken bone and a sardine tin to lick. I didn't realize the sun had dropped from the sky. I heard the brothers as they came up to our Main Bin.

"Rats in the trash!" said one.

"That's what's been taking our food!!" said the other. "Let's get 'im."

They both hooted and howled and next thing I knew we were all tipped over and the boys were fighting through the trash to get the rat. Which was me. About that time, fortunately for me, up came Marta and her mum. The boys and I rolled out of the bin, all covered in sticky filth. Marta giggled. So did her mum! This made the boys even angrier and they threw me on the sidewalk (ouch!) and sat glowering on the corner of the block.

Maybe that's the last time I heard Marta laugh. For sure it was the last time I raided the trash bin.

Marta's mum worked on the block with the brothers, taking sorted cardboard and plastics to other street dwellers called the Recyclers. Marta worked on the block going through trash bins, one after the other, and sorting out the easy stuff. She worked slower and slower and was coughing lots. Her face burned red with fever. Finally one morning she wouldn't wake up, no matter how much I licked her face and chewed on her ear.

Marta's mum picked her up, wrapped her in the one tattered blanket and asked a passerby for some change for the bus.

She said she was going to the Clinic in some part of the city far away. The brothers went, too. I was not invited. After they boarded the bus I sat by myself on the sidewalk, guarding the corner from first one and then another intruder—a boy with a sack, a girl with a shoulder bag, a snarling large dog (later I discovered his name was Bright Eye), and a policeman. Finally, after two bewildering days, the policeman made me leave.

"Go on, you mutt!" he growled—just like a mean dog. I didn't know what he meant, so I sat still, wagging my tail and turning my head a little, trying to catch the scent of what he said, but it didn't work.

He took a stick from his belt and shouted, "¡*Vete, go ON!*" and hit me alongside my ribs.

Ouch! I had no choice but to abandon my post—I had seen the soldiers with guns before, and this one was like a soldier. He told the baker that he should call the *Autoridades* if I returned and the baker nodded. Whoever that was, it sounded bad for me!

So, I skedaddled.

CHAPTER THREE

Scruffy Is Lost in the City

The problem was, I had no idea where to go. But I knew what I was looking for. I had only one goal, to find my Marta. First I headed straight up the path Marta's mum had taken on her way to the bus.

The sidewalk was crowded and it was hard to see upwards, but fortunately the signposts were higher than most of the heads of the people walking by. Finally, I saw a sign with a picture of a bus. I figured this was where Marta had gone. I waited, and waited, and finally along came a bus! I was one of the first aboard and the first to get thrown off. Not only was I a doggie, which turns out aren't permitted on buses, but I didn't have the silver pieces to give the driver.

I learned not to wait for the bus that took Marta away. Instead, I knew I must find her in the city, to listen for her voice amid the crowds and the many little voices floating above those cold streets, to catch a glimpse of her worn brown shoes or raggedy dress or shiny brown hair tied back into a little wispy tail.

I darted down alleys for shortcuts, over fences and down embankments and through vacant lots until finally I knew I was lost! I didn't know where that bus stop was nor did I have any idea where the old corner lay.

I wandered from one new corner to the next—I never was very good with directions. And it was so cold! I had nothing to eat and nowhere to rest out of the rain. I had nobody to talk to or play with, either. I cried a little, but that just made me tired, so I found some comfort curling into a ball, nose under tail. I dreamed I was curled next to my Marta.

I missed her lots, sometimes I thought I'd see her standing in her old torn blue dress and saggy leggings under a roof awning or her mum's umbrella, but I was always mistaken and often chased away when I went to say hello. Nobody needed a hungry little doggie, not when food was scarce enough for all concerned.

CHAPTER FOUR

Scruffy Joins a Gang

That's when I began to notice the Other Dogs. Some traveled alone, running from garbage pile to garbage pile, sniffing out what they could eat to survive. These were usually the tall dogs, large but skinny.

Others traveled in packs comprised of many sizes, except none so little as me. Further observations revealed no other little loner dogs like me on the street. One dog stood out from the rest of the pack leaders. He was called Bright Eye—so named because one of his eyes was milky white from a long-ago tussle.

He was a grouchy guy, maybe because he couldn't see very well.

But he was tough, real tough. He made his way with a bunch of less tough doggies to work the street corners, the garbage piles and restaurant backdoors, to eat a good living. He had a system so everybody could be well fed, have friends, and be happy! I noticed that none of the doggies in his band were as skinny as me. I decided to apply for membership.

My plan was to sit by the bench where one of Bright Eye's favorite garbage bins was situated. I could never get into that bin, because it was too high. Here, I figured, is where the brilliance of a gang came in! The big guys could help me get to the goods. Edible goods.

That's what made this system great, I thought, as I settled in to wait for the troops. I dreamed of sandwich ends, or bones from a steak, or even a yogurt carton. Mmmmm. I dreamed of myself on a rare sunny afternoon munching on a piece of bread. In my dream, a pesky kitten came over to beg a bite. I growled. The cat growled back!

I woke up in a hurry because somebody was truly growling at me! And there stood Bright Eye. King of the Bin. Whoops! I apologized profusely. He wasn't amused.

I rolled over onto my back to say, "Hey, really, I surrender and I'm not such a bad pup..." but he turned away. I slinked off to the back of his pack, where members gathered around. An old Poodle Gal winked at me and bid me to come sit by her. Bright Eye and the gang started snuffling through the garbage. Today they had good findings and the Top Dogs ate all around. Some of the gang stood on the fringes and growled at passersby, especially at other dogs—to allow Bright Eye and his toughs a serene meal.

Meanwhile, I was hungry from my dream and from watching those guys have their meal—I waited for any tiny scrap, wondering if this great system could work for me, too. But it didn't.

It seems I did not have the credentials to join Bright Eye. What could they be? The Poodle Gal, one of the skinnier of the guard faction, with wild, frizzy, matted fur, spoke out of the side of her mouth as she passed by.

"Stick around, little girlie—just keep to your own business and don't worry anybody here. Act like a guard! You'll end up with a scrap now and again."

So I stuck around. This was the only advice I'd gotten since being on my own. A "scrap now and again" sounded pretty darn good right about now. But if the *Autoridades* hadn't

eventually gathered up half the gang to which I was applying, I might have died of hunger in no time at all. And the only scraps were those I got from the Poodle Gal. She couldn't spare one bite from the looks of her, but she tossed me crumbs anyway. Meanwhile, I tried to prove to Bright Eye I had something to offer him and his gang.

On a typical sodden afternoon, I waited at the back of the pack, trying to look like I was helping and waiting for the scrap that rarely arrived. We were grouped around the best bin in town, where Tony Roma's rib bones were deposited. Why anyone would throw away perfectly good food was always a mystery to me. Anyway, somebody must have called the whistle on us, 'cause next thing you know, *Los Autoridades* had arrived.

It was a mean vehicle from the streets, full of crawling vermin, climbing out of the vehicle with nets, and wearing masks, thick rubber gloves and boots to the knees. They collect any of us who happen to be in their way and toss us into the back of the vehicle half-full of creatures captured elsewhere. From stories I've heard, it's a real Hell, 'cause newly tossed critters are set upon by those picked up earlier in the day. It's not unusual to be thrown into a mosh pit of crazed doggies, cats, sometimes even rats, chickens and goats—mostly alive, some dead.

Lucky for me, I was at the end of the line on the feeding chain, as usual.

I was slinking away down the alley but looked behind in surprise to see so many of the gang tossed into the back of the vehicle from

Hell. Last I saw, one of the masked guys was heading for Bright Eye himself. I watched as Bright Eye ducked the noose and let it settle over the Poodle Gal.

Wow. So much for leadership. He was just out for himself! That was it for me and gangs. And I felt very sorry for the Poodle Gal, the only living being who'd shown me any kindness in the last few weeks.

Once more, I skedaddled!

CHAPTER FIVE

Scruffy in Barrio Rosales

The world turned even drearier after those days with Bright Eye. Winter in the city was grey, cold, and wet. No food could be found in my world. Soon I didn't even care about that; I just wanted somewhere to lie down and rest. But a safe place to lie down was hard to come by.

Just when I thought I'd found a corner and had settled down for a nap, along comes a supplanter. That could be an *Autoridade* in a policeman's costume or a large stray dog. Or a person on a bicycle. Once in a while, a very mean cat. So, I trotted around the city. Soon I was only walking this way and that, trying to find a spot to rest.

My throat was sore from swallowing what food scraps I found. Even drinking water was painful. Crossing roads was scary and I waited hours and hours for the traffic noise to die down so I could cross in the dark, quieter hours of the night.

Sometimes I found a relatively tranquil alley but alleys had very different lives on different days and I couldn't count on any of them remaining quiet and peaceful for long. Plus, there was the rain. Oh, those were soggy days! Rain, more rain—this was bad enough. But then there were the booms and crashes and bright flashes, *thunder and lightning* I later learned. But I only remembered the night the soldiers came to our little farm—and I panicked and ran crying across the crowded streets on my very confusing journey. Looking back, it's a miracle I didn't get run over by a car on the slick streets of the city.

Then I discovered the residential section of *Barrio Rosales*. I recognized a quiet place, a building from my days with Marta and her mummy—where people would go to listen to the wise man and smell the sweet burning smoking sticks and listen to the chanting children. I slept for one night in the front alcove, away from the rain for an entire night. By morning I was dry, though still cold. Then up the stairs came a man wearing long robes who reminded me of the shamans who visited the family in the big stall—in our village below *Nevado del Huilla*.

He held rusty keys that took some time to fit in the keyhole of the old wooden door. I shrank back into the darkness of my alcove but I must have whimpered because he startled and turned around to look at me. I cringed, expecting to be hit with his stick. Yet he didn't frown, scowl or growl. Instead, he smiled. He reached into his robe pocket and pulled out a package wrapped in a napkin.

"*Yo soy el Padre Miguel*, I am Father Miguel. *¿Quién eres tú?* And you are...?" He held out his hand with a morsel. His words were melodic, like a prayer.

He offered me a piece of meat! Wow, I couldn't believe my luck. I licked it off his open hand. Still smiling, he opened the heavy wood door and went inside. I was so happy! Food and kindness, all in one

instance! I'm not sure which made me happier. Anyway, for a little while I had a warm feeling in my heart and my tummy. My throat burned from swallowing the meat. I slept again.

The next morning, I awoke to find many people climbing the steps toward my spot. The door swung open from the inside, and all these people filed into the building. Even though I shrank into the shadows, I was spotted by a few.

One little boy tried to give me a pat, but he reminded me of Marta's brothers and I shied away with a scaredy-cat whimper. His papa said he must now go and wash his hand and said something to a guy standing by the door, who then came over and gave me a swift kick. Ouch! I tried to turn my back but the boot headed in my direction again and caught me in my skinny spine. I yelped and ran down the steps into the yard and out onto the sidewalk.

I looked for another dry spot. Being scared gave me energy and I ran up one road and down another. Finally, I came to a quiet street and headed up the sidewalk which curved beyond my sight. This street wasn't too far from a store I remembered from my bin-raiding days with Bright Eye and the Gang. Whew, I was tired 'cause it was uphill!

But just in time, what do you know? Between one tall building and the next, I found a vacant lot—grass, trees, some bushes—and only closed off by a few skimpy strands of wire! I snuck under the bottom strand and headed up the slope of the lot. This was a temporary heaven. I curled up next to a tree and quickly fell asleep.

~ Chapter Six ~

Scruffy Finds A Friend

I poked my head out of a thicket of grasses at the foot of a tall tree. This was a rare sunny morning in winter when the clouds parted to allow the blessings of sunlight to warm chilled bones, flesh and earth. I licked some drops of water from a branch, whimpered, then rested my head on the lower branch to look outside my little nest. I was a very tired little doggie after so many days of trials and misfortunes.

I spotted a man coming over to investigate and thumpety-thumped my tail in the soggy leaves. Was he a nice man or a mean man? I didn't know. But I didn't move or try to get up. I didn't have the energy. The man knelt down to examine me. Hopeful that this man would help me, my tail thumpety-thumped even harder. He patted my sides, no doubt noticing I was all skin and bones—ribs sticking out of my matted fur. I had no strength to even move.

"Pobrecita—supongo que tienes un poco de hambre, ¿no?" said the man—he knew hunger when he saw it. He pulled out a sandwich from his knapsack, though this food might have come too late. He broke off half and held it out to me.

My little tongue licked my lips, but I barely had the strength to take hold of the sandwich. However, my tail thumped away in response. I was very grateful for the kindness. Then he broke off little pieces of the sandwich and fed them to me, one by one. I ate one, then another, then another. I struggled to my feet but yipped in pain and bit at my ribcage. Something was wrong—oh, yes, the man with the stick and the kicks. That was when the man lightly examined my wound, careful not to hurt me.

I squeaked a little "thank you" then turned in some circles and settled into my nest and laid my head back down for a rest. Whew! I had some hope now, lying there in the sun, having eaten some food. That evening the kind man stopped by once again with a fluffy rag to scrunch around me.

This went on for a few days. And for a few days, the rains held off—virtually a miracle in the city, I've been told.

Slowly I got stronger and my sore sides and wounds began to heal. But the cold deepened and the rains began again. And once again, I could not stop shivering and my cough became worse. The man with food did not come by for several days, but I was too tired to care.

Oh, it was terrible! The thunder and lightning reminded me of the soldiers on the farm. Every time I coughed, my side hurt, plus the coughing took all my energy. Then I started shivering from cold and, well, I was in a bad way. My little blanket from the man with food was soaked, the leaves under me were soaked, and the bush in which I lived was soaked. The rain just kept coming down.

My bright idea, on a day when I was hungrier than sick and sore, was to find my new, kind friend with the food! Maybe he had another piece of sandwich! I especially liked the ones with cheese, 'cause they didn't hurt my throat. So, I made my way down the sloping lot to the sidewalk which had brought me there in the first place. I looked up the hill, where the man always made his way. Oh my! This was quite a hill! This wouldn't be easy! But I was a bit desperate and so put my head down against the rain and pushed my way straight up with determination.

What I found was a bunch of parked Noise Machines, but at least they were quiet and had closed doors. Plus, tunnels that led to more cars. I guessed they were resting. People went in and out of doors to little caves. At the top of the road was the tallest, proudest building, like a castle.

But I found no friend with food. I looked for him, peering toward windows on the floor with the main door. If I leaned in off the street just a few inches I could get out of the rain. And so I did. I took a good nap, sitting up at first and then curled into the smallest size I could manage and still stay out of the rain. I couldn't stop shivering.

I awoke to the sound of one of those Noise Machines arriving at the gate where I was curled up. In fright, I pulled back into the shadow of the overhang but the gate I leaned on began to open. The car (I learned the word later in School) was coming forward. In a panic I darted inside, following the opening door. I hid in a corner as the car pulled against the wall. I was in a concrete tunnel with lots of cars and bicycles, all resting. The floor, walls, and objects were all dark and cold.

I could see the end of all my days. I was too tired to care. Maybe instead of a piece of sandwich I just needed to sleep!

A glimmer of light flickering from the far end proved to be an open door, so I skedaddled through it. I stepped outside once again, this time into a beautiful garden, like the vacant lot, but cared for. I was excited. A bin here must be worth searching through! After some exhausting investigation, I realized there was no bin. I couldn't get out of the rain anywhere here either, and vines and metal stakes made it really hard to move, especially with my very sore ribs.

I had to rest and curled up under the thickest bush I could find. I couldn't think straight and just wanted to sleep. I shut my tired eyes. A golden warmth beckoned and I recognized the blurry figure of a little girl wearing a ragged blue dress. I just wanted to curl up and sleep; never mind the rain, never mind my sore throat, never mind my sore, festering sides. Just sleep now. Ah, I could see the birds from the farm soaring high into a clear, blue sky. Flying high, spiraling on gentle winds.

Later, the man who gave me the sandwich and saved me again, Luis, the *portero* of the apartment building, *Altos del Castillo*, told me his story. He, like me, once lived on a farm!

Luis walked to and from work from his bus stop on Avenida 7. His path led him past the vacant lot on Calle 71, where he'd found me. Over the years he'd seen all the vacant lots turned into high-rise buildings for rich people and he was glad to see at least one remaining holdout; the lot stayed empty, not sold to builders.

Luis had grown up on a farm in the south and loved the open spaces and the gifts of nature including birds, butterflies and wildflowers. He grew up with calves, burros, chicks, even kitties and puppies. He missed those sights, sounds and smells, but life was lean in the countryside, and the violence inescapable and increasing, so he arrived in the city years before to earn a better living for his family.

One day, he passed the vacant lot and saw a small furry head pop up. That head was mine!

Thus, Luis told me how he found me, not that I understood the story exactly, 'cause I hadn't been to School yet, but he was watching his security monitor as a car pulled into the garage. He was required to watch each and every vehicle, to make sure no funny business went on. It didn't sound very funny to me, because he said a car with a bomb destroyed *Club El Nogal* down the street, and many people had died.

He was surprised to see me limp into the building, sneaking in next to the car! He was sorry to watch me entering the back garden.

"*¡Carumba!*" now he had to do something about it, since he had very strict rules. In fact, his instructions from the Garden Committee were to call the *Autoridades*! He knew what would happen to me if they arrived.

So, he thought. He ate his sandwich. He thought some more.

Maybe first he could catch the critter (me), then he could decide what to do.

All I wanted was to sleep, because my dream was so lovely and there I found warmth. But somebody was trying to pull me away from my dream and I moved closer to the next tree and got tangled in vines. Maybe here nobody would bother me. I didn't know Luis was pulling his way up close to the tree by the same vines I thought would hide me. I moved further away. My dream returned. I rested, knowing I'd soon be back in the sunshine with my friends. Somehow, I was drawn back to my beloved Marta and the beckoning sunshine from the farm in *Nevado del Huilla*.

Suddenly a man was coming toward me under the trees and bush. He had on a uniform! I remembered all too well the soldiers and my brother Carlitos' quick end of days. Whimpering, I tried to escape but could only move slowly 'cause I was so cold.

Slipping, I found refuge under a bush but the soldier came toward me again. Everything blurred—I tried to find a path but instead tumbled and skidded on slick leaves, down, down toward a rushing stream. I landed on a ledge, shaking, just wanting to return to my dream. Then, I felt something settle over my neck, and I was pulled up high, toward the skies—and I didn't care what happened next. I resigned myself to ending my search for my Marta forever, and ending my days.

But Luis let go. He knew it would take some time for me to get used to the rope. He went back to his desk to have some coffee and to think. The elevator opened, and out stepped the Foreigner Lady. She greeted Luis, stiffly as usual, then saw the rope.

"What's going on?" she asked in her accented Spanish.

"*Me entró un perro,*" answered Luis. A light went on in Luis's mind! This was the lady who petted all the building's spoiled dogs!

"A small doggie snuck into the garden, *¿Pudiera Ud. ayudarme en atraparla? Can you help me?"*

She frowned, hesitating. Then, "*Tal vez. No tengo prisa hoy, que es Domingo*, I was just going shopping, no meetings."

So out came Luis and the lady. Luis continued to walk toward me until I was backed into a corner between the drainage ditch and the wall. That's when I stumbled and fell onto a ledge above the ditch with fast flowing water.

Now the lady leaned forward frowning and fists clenched! Luis lowered the rope to the ledge in the drainage ditch where I was hunched and shivering, with my eyes closed. A dirty river rushed just below the ledge. He got the rope and pulled it tight and hauled me out of the ravine. I hung limply at the end of the rope.

"*¿Y ya que?*"asked the lady. "Now what?"

"*Tengo que llamar Los Autoridades,*" said Luis, as he struggled down the embankment, dragging me behind him on the rope. As he bent to pick me up, a very soggy doggie, he looked up at the Foreigner Lady. *"Asi son las reglas."*

The Foreigner Lady frowned harder—she was not accustomed to being told what the rules were.

"*Primero,* I will dry her off," said the Lady. Without comment or expression Luis held out the doggie (me).

"She's shivering!" said the lady.

"She's hungry," said Luis.

That was the beginning of my new life, but I didn't know it at the time. I was half fainting with the exhaustion of all these efforts and could barely think. All I remember is somebody putting a cloth around me and carrying me.

A ringing took over my little head and some bright lights flashed, like many suns, and I heard Marta giggling. But that day faded into oblivion and I remembered little else.

CHAPTER SEVEN

Scruffy Moves to the High Castle

I must have slept for a very long time. The Foreigner Lady handed me to a girl, Consuelo, who worked in her house and I heard some murmuring human voices. Then I was put on top of a bunch of cloth, covered up with some really soft warm blankets pulled out of a big metal machine.

I woke up thirsty. Just in front of me was a bowl of water and a little food on a tray. I couldn't believe my luck! I drank lots but didn't eat because my throat was too sore for swallowing. I snuggled into my little bed and sank back into dreams.

Unfortunately, the dreams didn't last long enough. Consuelo, the housekeeper, decided I was too dirty to be allowed into the rest of the house until after I'd had a *BATH!* I knew nothing about baths but found out soon enough. She took me into the room with noisy machines and warm cloths and put me in a basin. I started shivering again! Next thing I knew, water and smelly gooey stuff was poured all over me. I cried and wiggled out of Consuelo's hands but she picked me right up again and plopped me back into the water. It was terrible!

At last I was dried off and brought into the Foreigner Lady's room. A fire was crackling in the corner. Consuelo put a pillow next to the fire and I settled down to rest, exhausted again from the latest struggle. The Foreigner Lady looked at me briefly, but then resumed scratching on the papers on her desk.

I felt some itching. Soon I felt lots of itching and began to squirm. I bit at my fur because my fur was biting me! Little black dots hopped off my forehead onto my nose and then onto the floor. Oh! I was suddenly miserable 'cause I felt like a thousand nettles were stinging me all at once.

Consuelo came in with tea for the Foreigner Lady. She looked over at me and shrieked and jumped. They both came over to check me out. I whimpered and tried to make myself smaller. Maybe I would get kicked again! Something was bad!

"*Pulgas*," said Consuelo.

"Yes, fleas," said the Foreigner Lady.

"*Están saltando por todas partes,*" said Consuelo.

The Foreigner Lady nodded, "They'll soon be everywhere!" She picked up the phone, and in no time at all the *Mesenjero* was at our door with a bottle. The sight of the bottle made me uneasy. It turned out to be a bottle of Flea Bath.

Yes, time for another bath. I'd gone from never having a bath before in my life to having two baths in less than a few hours. After my second bath, which I objected to strenuously, I was so tired I went back to sleep. When I woke up I was given bread soaked in warm milk with honey. A warm glow fanned a flame in my heart. Nobody was going to kick me, after all!

- CHAPTER EIGHT -

Scruffy Finds A Home. And A Name.

So, thanks to Luis, the man with the food, I now had a Home. We lived in a proud building called *Altos del Castillo,* the High Castle, at the top of a very fancy street. We lived on the very top floor of the top building on the fancy street. But even better, I had new friends: Luis, Consuelo, and the Foreigner Lady. Well, she wasn't too friendly at first but Luis told me she was sad, lonely, and scared in Colombia, and had few friends.

She did not want a pet—not even a cat but especially not a dog. Back home in another country she had a farm and a dog and some horses and she missed them more than she could say. She missed the scrub oaks and wildflowers sparkling like bright colorful stars on a sandy sky. She missed her husband who had left her alone in this foreign land after their daughter died. And of course, most of all, she missed her little girl, whom she would never see again in this life. This lady was shrouded in a longing born of sorrow born of loss. It hung over her like the soggy days when I was lost on the cold concrete sidewalks in Bogota.

She was a little grouchy but gave me really good food and took me to the lady doctor who gave me an examination, some pills, and some shots. Of course, since I'm a crybaby, I whimpered a little at the shots, but my sore throat went away in a few days so I was pretty happy.

The lady, my new mummy as it turned out, told Consuelo my name was to be Scruffy. That's how I became Scruffy. Later, my mummy told me that I was called Scruffy because I was (and am) scruffy. I'm not sure what that word means, except I know I come from raggedy stock.

Anyway, life changed and how. Little by little, I became a Strong Doggie. And soon I even had toys! First was a little bear my mummy bought when she was buying more Flea Soap. Then a plastic ring from the lady doctor's store. And as soon as the doctor said I was healthy enough, I began to go on walks.

Lots of rich people lived in my building. These people had rich dogs. These dogs went on walks. Oscar, the Dog Walker, came at 7:00 a.m. to take the rich dogs for walks in the park. One morning our doorbell rang. Mummy had just bought me a new ring to put around my neck—a collar—and a leash to tie to the ring.

"Consuelo!" she called out, "it's time for Scruffy's walk!"

I was really scared to go out that door. What if I got lost on the street again? Or was going to get another shot at the lady doctor's place? Or what if the man with the stick hit me? But, of course, I had to go. Consuelo handed the leash to Oscar and off I went.

But it wasn't so bad! I met Allegra, who lived on the floor below us. She was an okay gal—sort of silly, and not wise like the Poodle Gal. She was pretty though, with a bow in her hair, which was also silly because it hung over her eyes, so sometimes she bumped into things.

Out on the street was the world I used to know so well. But this time I was on a leash, which meant I didn't have to find my way because Oscar knew where we were going. I didn't have to be afraid of the guy with the stick because I was on a leash! I didn't have to look out for traffic because on my leash, Oscar kept me out of traffic! On a leash! It was great! And I wasn't lonely on these streets because I was walking with Allegra. Maybe I should say *strolling* with Allegra. She did not have a lot of energy because she was a bit fat so we spent lots of time sniffing things. On the leashes, of course.

Finally, my mummy told me I didn't have to worry about getting lost (actually, she said she didn't have to worry about losing me) because I had one of the silver jangly pieces on my ring that told people where I lived. Life had changed for me, indeed.

I started to look forward to the doorbell at 7:00 a.m. when Consuelo handed me over to Oscar, and Allegra and I walked the streets and parks of Barrio Rosales on leashes. During the day I played outside on the two *terrazas* where Consuelo grew herbs. In the evening Consuelo, or sometimes even my new mummy, would take me out again. I was proud to be on that leash, I had an Owner, on the mean streets where I'd once been so lost.

CHAPTER NINE

Still Searching

But even in the luxurious *Barrio Rosales* were street corners on which raggedy people lived. My new mummy said they were *desplazados*, driven from their homes to a hard life in the city because of war in the countryside. They worked the streets the same way my old family and I used to—sorting bins of trash and recycling, looking for food and for cardboard boxes to live in. One day I was walking down the Rosales hill with dear Allegra, when lo, I spied two boys and a little girl sorting through trash. The little girl wore a raggedy blue dress, and her tangled brown hair was pulled back with a ribbon.

"Marta!" I yipped, tearing out of Oscar's grasp and rushing straight for the little girl. I hopped up and licked her face—but it wasn't Marta at all. At first, she shrieked in frightened surprise, but then broke into a huge smile and then, gales of giggles. She scratched my head and kissed my nose. I kissed back, naturally.

Oscar yanked my leash and pulled me back into line and of course, we marched off. The little girl shouted goodbye and blew me kisses. This would have been the end of that story except next time it was my new mummy who walked me around the same block where this little girl worked in the trash. She saw me first. Her face lit up and she held out her hands so of course, I made a beeline for a hug. She wasn't my Marta, but she smelled and looked almost the same. My mummy was surprised and dropped the leash, but I didn't notice because I was getting big hugs from this little girl.

"*¿Como se llama la perrita?*" asked the girl. "What is the doggie's name?"

"*Se llama Scruffy,*" said my mum.

"*Scwaffy,*" said the girl.

"*Scruffy,*" said my mum.

The girl nodded in agreement. "*Scwaffy!*"

"*Nos disculpa*—excuse us," said my mum as she picked up my leash and off we went.

But that wasn't the end! From then on, whenever we went around that corner, there was my new friend! And her little brother, and her mum, and sometimes her cousins.

"*SCWAFFY*" they would shriek and come running and ask my mummy if they could run in the park with me. At first Mummy said no, but then she said yes, and I would get one or two laps around the merry-go-round with all the kids running and laughing, tumbling over each other and sometimes me.

Mummy talked to *La Señora* while we were running around the merry-go-round. She watched the little girls and boys dressed in torn and dirty clothing, but so happy with a chance to play with raggedy me. She watched and watched but then we would abruptly head home.

CHAPTER TEN

Off the Leash! But Not Lost

And so it went. Amazing how in an instant my luck had changed. To have a home—and not in a barn, not on a cold street, not next to a trash bin. To have friends: Allegra, the kids in the park, Consuelo, Oscar, and of course Luis, who seemed almost as delighted with my new life as I was.

But best of all was to have my new mummy, even if she was a bit glum. I figured out how to make her smile by crawling on my belly and growling at my toys, by chewing up the toys she'd bought and burying them under her pillow, by leaping high into the air—almost as high as her face—when she walked through the door after her day at the office. Okay, at first maybe she was annoyed and would say "*Vete,*" but I would not give up, even though sometimes she would.

"*¡Vete! ¡Ábrese! ¡Ay! CONSUELO,*" who came running to give me a biscuit and lure me off into the kitchen, which wasn't a bad thing.

I loved my walks. Never mind that at first they were scary because of the long days I was lost and wandering the streets after I misplaced my home corner and family. But when I was out on the leash with Oscar I felt so safe! Instead of looming with scary possibilities, the streets became downright interesting. First, were the little kids I made friends with on my travels around the blocks and into the parks. But I had other delightful moments chasing little birds out of the bushes, and the frogs by the stream, not to mention the rats! I would ALMOST get them, but they were just too fast for me. But only slightly, and I knew with more practice I would soon succeed.

One day in the park where other dogs and their masters were hanging out, mummies gossiping with other mummies, and *empleadas* recounting tales with other *empleadas,* Oscar decided to let me roam free. That means he unclipped my collar from my leash! Oh no! I whimpered and tried to lie down on his feet. He booted me off. Then I tried to jump up into his arms, but he kept them folded. I noticed he was smiling.

"*¡Corre, corre, Scrufficita!* Run!" he commanded. But I wasn't so sure.

Then I saw a jolly, red-coated, long-haired fellow chasing a ball. That looked kind of fun! I ran over to say hello and to see if I could play, too, the way I did with the kids at the playground. He did NOT want to share! He growled a little, good naturedly, not like Bright Eye, and ran as fast as he could away from me. I felt really sad.

"Scruffy" I heard Oscar shout, "*¡ven acá, mira!*" And lo, Oscar had a bright green ball in his hand. He threw it towards me, and I pounced! This time I caught the critter. YAY! I felt so cool and galloped around the park with my head held high, my trophy ball in my jaws. Then the red-coated dog saw me with MY ball and came running at me. At first I was scared, but then I saw he had his OWN ball. He just wanted to run with me, so we steamed around the park at full speed—around and around. And around. It was like flying. I remembered the beautiful birds from the farm.

The other dog's name was Rojo and we became fast friends!

CHAPTER ELEVEN

Scruffy Goes to School

Autumn returned to Bogota and as the cold set in I remembered again my little friend who kept me warm on our journey down the mountain when we left the farm forever. She was my sister, my companion, and I still missed her. In fact, not a day went by that I didn't imagine I'd hear her giggles at one of our jokes (like her sneaking a crust for me!), or see her raggedy blue dress flouncing as she played hopscotch on the sidewalk, or listen to a little tune she sang when we worked the bins.

Sometimes when I drowsed in the noonday sun on our *terraza* I imagined the sweet little body that kept me warm on bitter nights. But it was the sunshine from the sky that seeped into my bones, not the warmth from my little Marta. As I woke up my memory lost the essence of her being and she faded back to a longing that finally settled into a deep place in my own little heart.

Nonetheless, my days became increasingly pleasant. I played with the kids at the playground, walked with Allegra and Oscar and sometimes my mummy, and chased balls with my new friend Rojo at the park. My fear of being lost on the streets went away. In fact, it became unthinkable: I had a home, a little bed, Consuelo, my new mummy, and my new friends. That was my new life, although I knew deep down that everything could change again in an instant.

And of course, it did. But I'll get to that later.

Mummy began to bring "stuff" on our walks, and sometimes Consuelo had to come along to help carry "stuff." While I played with the playground kids, Mummy and Consuelo consulted with the parents, the older brothers and sisters, aunts and uncles. She handed out "stuff." And as the days got colder, I noticed that the kids had sweaters and coats. They also carried books and lunch boxes—this was new! And sometimes, instead of running over to play, they sat on the bench, writing in a book, scratching on papers. Sometimes Consuelo sat with them and listened to their words or looked at their scratchings.

They were going to School! The reason I knew about School was because I, too, was going to School. That started after I ran across a street chasing a ball and Mummy shrieked.

"SCRUFFY, STAY!!" I didn't stay because I didn't know what "stay" meant! And the cars going by were honking and screeching and Mummy says I almost got hit and she was so mad she was shaking and crying. She said I had to learn to behave!

So I had to go to School to learn how to "stay," but it didn't stop there—I also learned "come," "*vente*," "*siéntate*," "sit down" and the like. I became bilingual, Mummy said. I also learned "*dame tu pata*" and "shake!" This is behaving. And when I watched the children doing their homework instead of playing, I saw that this is how they learned to behave. They won't get hit by any cars either.

But it made me a little sad, because I wondered whether if Marta had learned to behave, maybe she wouldn't have become so ill and have to go away on the bus. Maybe I wouldn't have lost my corner and my family and my sister, my friend.

Well, I learned to have new sisters and friends, but I still always look for Marta on all my walks and travels.

Chapter Twelve

Mummy Brings Home a Basket

Something was going on at our house. Consuelo was cleaning out closets. Luis was hauling stuff up from the storage locker. Consuelo put things in cardboard cartons. Lots of stuff was hauled away for trash, stuff was given to our families on the corners. Mummy met with Father Miguel and they scratched things on paper, making plans.

The *Mesenjero* arrived with some Supplies, including a funny basket with a door and holes on the side with bars. Consuelo put my food inside the basket! And my water, too! I was hungry after a few days because I was not going into that basket to eat. I might never get out! I got thirsty, too.

Oscar still arrived every morning at 7:00 a.m. but he looked glum and gave me lots of pats. I ran out of energy because I wasn't eating so our walks were slow, which was just fine with Allegra. Finally I had to eat something so I stuck my head as far as I could in the basket and licked some biscuits out of the little dish.

Meanwhile, we went to some Celebrations. One was at night at the *residencia del Embajador*, a couple were *almuerzos*, during the day, with lots of food from hot grills in back of houses with their own parks. Mummy took me along except the one at the Embassy, where she worked. Doggies weren't allowed past Security because we could be Terrorist Doggies. Since my mum was the Mission Director for a company called USAID, the final party was held at a very fine restaurant up on one of the hills in La Calera. That was the last party and then apparently everyone was going away. I did not look forward to that final party.

For now, Mummy hummed and sang lots of the time, which is different than my mum used to be. Even Consuelo seemed happy—she packed her own bags and talked about living a whole new life on my mummy's farm! Well that really scared me 'cause I realized I might be losing not just my mummy, but my Consuelo as well. My life at *Altos del Castillo* seemed to be coming to an end.

Everything was in a big uproar, including me. Oscar still arrived everyday, Consuelo still took me for flea baths, and I now ate my meals inside the silly basket. But all the closets were empty, we had many boxes stacked up, and even all my toys were put away. Something wasn't right! I became a little nervous. No, a lot nervous.

One day a bunch of guys came along and took all the boxes, and most of the furniture, even my special doggie bed (on which I never slept, but it was fun to chew on and toss about) and my little haven became very bare.

I was so happy for so long and everything seemed sunny and bright in my life. But I knew better. I knew what it was to feel lost and lonely and sad, when everything you thought was yours forever was suddenly taken away. It made me glad I'd had so much fun with my new mummy and my new family on the corners where we walked, and with my Walker, Oscar, and my Doorman (and Rescuer), Luis and even silly Allegra. I knew I would remember all that love and all that fun for the rest of my years. I was glad that at least once in my life I'd been a Lucky Doggie. But my heart was heavy so my head hung low, and my tail, too. I knew that once things started getting sad they just kept getting sadder 'cause that had happened to me before. I was afraid. *Tenía miedo*. And so, I became even more afraid.

When we went outside late that evening to get into the big car with Mummy's driver, Luis stopped me at the door. He picked me up and gave me such a squeeze, I thought maybe he was going away somewhere, too, and I would not see him again so I licked and licked his face and cried a little because I would miss him. I thanked him for his sandwiches when I was alone and hungry and I thanked him for pulling me out of the ditch and for giving me a new mummy and a Home.

CHAPTER THIRTEEN

Finding an Old Friend

We were on our way up to La Calera in the Range Rover, the big car, on windy cobblestone streets that climbed the little hill—past the *talleres*, past the rustic stables where people kept horses for riding or for pulling carts, past the bars with horses tied to posts outside the door (which Mummy said was good because the people did not have to worry about drinking and driving, whatever that means).

We went up and up and up to the top of the hill, to the restaurant that overlooked the entire city, where you could see the lights twinkling like stars and you imagined that each one was a house or a corner with a lantern, all with families who had warm clothes and were happy and healthy and went to School and maybe had a doggie and maybe would stay like that forever.

We sat down at a large table, Mummy at the front, and with lots of people in fancy clothes, women in long gowns that glittered like the stars in the night sky. They sat and talked about many things —mostly about my mummy, and about missing her when she was gone. Turns out we were at a Final Farewell Party. Someone laughed at me, calling me the Terrorist Doggie, but I didn't get the joke.

Even though I started out on Mummy's lap, I ended up on a chair of my own because she had to stand up to make a little chat here, a thank you there, a toast to her colleagues.

At first she held me in her arms as she talked, but I was too wiggly and she spilled her wine. She put me on a chair and told me to "*siéntate*," one of the things I learned in School—to sit and be quiet. She seemed happy and her eyes were bright when she talked about returning to California.

I was a little sleepy, because riding in the car was exhausting and watching all the box packing was exhausting, and I was already missing Luis, who seemed to be going away. I lay down on my very own chair which was pulled to one side near the edge of the outdoor terrace. I looked out over the village below, still high above the city lights. My eyes wandered across the yards and houses of La Calera—some with children playing out back, many with chickens and goats and some with little stalls and small yards or small barns. All were humble, but almost none were shacks.

Then I saw the burro. He was happily munching hay, ignoring the chicken sitting on his back and the kittens chasing his switching tail. A flicker of remembrance…a memory flashed from long ago.

Jacobo! I couldn't believe my own eyes—in a flash I hopped down from the chair and onto the terraza. I stared into the yard, far down the hill. Yes, it was Jacobo! I skedaddled down the hill, tearing through overgrown brush with no real path, heading straight for the light of that stable.

I crossed the old cobblestone road, running, running toward that little stall! And then, there he was in front of me, grey, furry, brown-eyed, lop-eared, and good humored as always. When he saw me, he jumped a little, because I was yipping and jumping and biting his feet and licking his nose and I think I even bit his floppy ears. I rolled over on my back, wagged my tail, crying from pure delight. The chickens scattered, shrieking and the kittens hissed and backed up, but not too far. Jacobo looked down at me (I know, I was acting like a silly dog who had never been to School at all) but finally he caught the scent. He gave me a nudge with his big, soft, whiskered nose.

"So it's you," he said, and he chortled in his donkey way, which is noisy and can cause quite a commotion. The kittens hissed louder, the chickens cackled and squawked and somebody came running from the big stall across from Jacobo's stall.

"So it's you!!" I said, but in such a whimper that nobody could tell what I meant to say, and I couldn't stop crying, but out of sheer joy, not one drop of sadness.

"You are alive!!" But I didn't need to say that, because not only was he alive, he was a little bit fat! He was well-muscled, and his eyes were bright, not dull as when he'd walked away, following his New Owner.

"And you are alive and well too, I see," he said in his funny mumbling bray.

"Never thought I'd see you again!" we said at the same time.

But from the big stall someone came running, shrieking—oh, it was scary! It was a little girl, dressed in warm clothes, which is good, 'cause La Calera at nighttime is cold. "*¡Papá, vente, ladrones! ¡No le toques mi Jacobito!*" She was carrying a big stick, bigger than she was, and she was as mad as she was scared.

"Don't hurt him!" She was very small, but very scary. I shrunk as small as I could.

I whimpered, "But he's my friend!" Of course, she didn't understand doggie words, but she *could* see that I was also very little. So she dropped her stick. She came over to Jacobo, petted his nose, and pulled some *panella* from her pocket, whispering to Jacobo.

"Don't tell my daddy I'm giving you this…" and he licked up the sweet brown sugar, dropping some on the hay for me, which I lapped up. She laughed. "*Ah Jacobo, mi amor, siempre tan amable con las bestias.* But this is no beast," and she dropped to her knees, holding out her hand. "This is a very cute little doggie."

By then her papa arrived and he carried a gun. "*No te preoccupes, papi,*" she said—"*no es ladrón,* it's just a *cachorro,* a puppie!"

Meanwhile, I could not believe my luck—here was my old friend. Last time I saw him he seemed on his way to Doom, but now I saw that he was happy and healthy, and he had a Little Girl who loved him dearly enough to defend him with a stick.

I wanted to hear his story! But I didn't have a chance. Her papa told her she must return to the house and to please send the mama, because they would have to decide what to do about the *cachorro.*

And not to worry, nothing would happen to her beloved Jacobo. He said that quietly, as if it was a decision made by someone other than himself. Jacobo was chuckling and munching hay. Then I realized I had no idea where the restaurant was, or my mummy. Oh no! Was I lost again?

Papa sat down on the bale of hay. He looked at me, and he looked at Jacobo.

"*¡Ay!*" was mainly what he kept saying. "*Pues, entonces ya tiene mi hija otra mascota*…not another pet to feed!" He held his hand out to me, which of course I licked. Mainly I wanted to hear the tale of Jacobo. But also, I knew I was lost again, and I sure didn't want to lose my new mummy!

I asked Jacobo if he knew where the fancy restaurant on the top of the hill might be. And Jacobo, being Jacobo, said well, maybe tomorrow we could find a *sendero* to take us up the hill. But now he was busy—he had a chicken on his back and hay to munch. I scrunched down on the straw, head on paws, with one tiny whimper.

Scruffy Isn't Lost, Was Never Lost

Then, just when the little girl and her mama came from their house to talk to the *Sr. Papá*, another big commotion began. Not just chickens cackling and kittens hissing—but a lone lead figure running through the brush, through rough branches that tore at her elegant gown. And following her, huffing and puffing, were people also running down a little narrow path, following the hill to the cobblestone road and across to the lighted stall. The papa, mama and little girl watched this stream of people in astonishment.

At the front of the pack was the person who told me I would never get lost again. There, in the door to the stable was my mummy, wearing her glittery long gown. Her face was shiny with tears. And behind her were all her Final Farewell Party Friends. No one in that group was dressed for a burro's stable, for sure. Their gowns and clothes sparkled like the lights of Barrio Rosales, not a barnyard lamp in La Calera.

"Don't hurt my doggie!" Mummy commanded. Her tone was fierce and she raised her hand in a fist! But then she scooped me up in shaky arms and gave me a big kiss. She didn't seem to mind that I was muddy from a barnyard. Behind her was the driver, and behind the driver was a soldier, with a gun as well. He looked at Jacobo, at the little girl, and at the little girl's father. The group in Fancy Clothes was speechless, at least for a moment.

"Seems to be a misunderstanding," said one of the men in fancy suits.

"*Parece que sea un amigo antiguo de Scruffy*," said the driver.

"It's just a burro," said my Mummy.

Everybody laughed. "No, that's a mule!" Well I didn't care, for me it was Jacobo and he was alive and well and happy—like me!

The papa said, "He was my pack mule, and he carried my tools. But he got old, and now I use my horse and a cart instead."

Mummy told me later that this meant his business was good, because a horse and cart are much more expensive than a simple burro carrying tools.

"But my *hija* loves him so, what could I do?" The papa continued the tale. "If I sold him or let him go wild in the hills then she would never stop crying. *Entonces*, he is our *mascota,* our pet! Besides, he is a good watch dog—he brays when robbers come by and defends the chickens and the geese with his hooves—better even than a dog with his teeth!!"

He had probably said this many times to convince even himself.

Somebody in the Fancy Crowd laughed, but everyone turned to him saying "Hush!" and then he was quiet.

Christine

- CHAPTER FIFTEEN -

Goodbye, and the Sum of It All

Mummy said later that *Sr. Papá*, the father, was just trying to prove he wasn't silly keeping an animal no longer able to bear a burden—no longer "economically useful." But I knew better, 'cause I knew Jacobo, and I know his heart is as big as the mountains in *Nevado del Huilla*. And I knew the father's tale was true—'cause it's all about loving a little girl and wanting to give her everything good in the world.

I also know how it feels to be loved by someone who wants to give you everything good in the world, which is my new mummy. I knew then that she wasn't leaving me alone in the city where I was once so lost. She would take me with her. Because she cared enough to run across the cobblestone road in her very fine clothes to a humble stable. Before that she had sent me to School, put jangles on my neck ring so I was never lost, held me close to her heart when she thought she had lost me but then found me again. Her heart thumped like thunder, like the booming shots fired by soldiers.

So I said my goodbyes to Jacobo. He gave me as big a hug as a burro can and as I left, carried by my mummy, I saw the kittens once again chasing his tail and biting the tasseled end, and a hen sitting on Jacobo's back. Young chicks picked up pieces of grain dropped from the hay that Jacobo chewed.

The little girl, her papa and mama waved goodbye, still hardly believing their eyes as our glittery group made its way back up the hill.

The old days are always here, with me—even as my own circumstances change. The present days of life march on into the future days, but past days, both the good and the bad, the joyful and the sad, remain. Sometimes it's hard to remember which came first, 'cause in the end, life's sum is a mix of all of those days.

That night we headed to my old new home in *Altos del Castillo*, the High Castle—and I, for one, slept soundly. Soon after, we went to a new home, in a new land, which is another story I will tell one day.

But for now my little doggie heart is lost in wonder of that sum of my own life, thus far.

The End of Book One

About the Author

Over the last three decades Susan Corning has worked in rural development across three continents: Latin America, Sub-Saharan Africa, and Asia. Her MSc from the College of Agriculture, University of Maryland, College Park gave her entrée into jobs that took her to faraway locales. These jobs, in turn, gave her unique immersion in multi-cultural environments where she worked alongside socio-economically marginalized people.

Places she has lived and worked include Colombia, Ecuador, Peru, Kenya, Uganda, Botswana, and South Africa. Her favorite animals include horses, dogs, elephants, cheetahs, giraffes, rock hyrax, and Ankole cattle.

Susan's hobbies include equestrian pursuits, raising hens, and gardening. Currently Susan lives on a farm in Bend, Oregon along with her husband Roger, three dogs, two cats, six horses, and 19 chickens. She still owns a horse in Ecuador, as well as one in Kenya.

About the Illustrator

Christine Eyer loves living in beautiful Bishop, California, where she enjoys painting, tending her creekside garden, and doting on her four rescue dogs.

About the Muse

The real Scruffy lives in Nairobi with Dieke, Scruffy and Susan's former horse trainer, who was able to coax a soul back into an abandoned pony, Zeus. That is a story for another day.

Illustrations by Christine Eyer

Published by
The Scruffy Saga Press
Bend, Oregon

www.thescruffysaga.com

ISBN 978-0-578-70833-1 (softcover)

ISBN 978-0-578-73968-7 (hardcover)

Book design by Lucky Valley Press
www.luckyvalleypress.com

Printed on acid-free paper